AMBER IN THE REAL WORLD

SAMUEL FLEMING

A VISIONARY SCI FI NOVELLA

Cover art by Diren Yardimli

Interior title art by MiblArt

ISBN-13: 978-1-954679-01-6 (paperback)
ISBN-13: 978-1-954679-00-9 (ebook)

Thank you to my Beta Readers

and to my First Reader,

Mel.

Contents

Part 1

Amber opened her Toyota's red door and carefully hopped into the driver's seat, smoothing out her purple sundress as she did. She started it up and ran the wipers to get the dew off the windshield. Then she drove the congested highway to the office.

Traffic already… slowing to a dead stop. She squeezed the steering wheel in frustration.

"Noah, is there a way around this?"

"There are no detours advised," her Artificial Assistant's voice said calmly through the speakers on the passenger side. Even though she knew that Noah wasn't a person, Amber always pictured him as a mid-twenties (like herself), well-dressed man. Dark hair, thin face, five o'clock shadow. Him speaking through the passenger speakers helped with the illusion.

Amber sighed and looked across the car, to the forest that lined the highway. It was only Tuesday and she was thinking too much again.

This couldn't be all there was to life. Wake up, get ready for work, go to work, come home, eat, sleep. Wait for the weekend: See her bestie, Bethany, get a date, occasionally like them enough to sleep with them but not enough to date them. See her folks once a month across the state. Sprinkles of holidays.

"You're stressing again," Noah said, almost like he was right beside her.

She groaned long, exasperated, and only slightly over-acted. "How could you tell?"

"You have audible and biometric cues."

She stared out at the vast sea of traffic. "It's just... There has to be more than this."

"Oh, that again," Noah replied flatly. "Have you thought anymore about painting? Classes are starting in two weeks at the community college."

Amber's shoulders sagged. She had thought about it. Painting would be one more hobby in a long line of hobbies that didn't help. They were just wallpaper over the metaphorical walls around her. It was the walls that were the problem.

It wasn't that they needed to be repainted or spackled. Even redoing the drywall wouldn't help. She wished she could tear down the walls. Tear down the whole house.

The house didn't feel right. The world didn't feel right.

"Is it that again?" Noah asked, knowing exactly what she was thinking—which wasn't hard, because the subject kept coming up. She used to talk to Noah a lot when she was alone at home, about a lot of different things. Lately they only talked about that.

Noah was the only one she could talk to about it. Bethany had laughed. Amber's parents thought she should see a counselor. Forget talking to the ladies at the office. She couldn't bring it up on a date—it wasn't exactly a date-conversation.

Her throat cinched. She felt so alone. "I refuse, Noah. I refuse to believe that this is all there is." Her voice cracked. "There has to be more."

Silence, except for the occasional honk and faint radios from the still sea of traffic. Amber gently wiped away a tear. She didn't want to smudge her make-up. She had already made that mistake once and fielded questions the rest of the day from the office ladies.

"What if you're right?" Noah said. "How would you feel?"

She chuckled. "I would say that I told you so." She looked over to the empty seat where Noah's voice came from. "I would probably cry. Then I would want to know what the world is really like."

Silence, even from outside. No honks, no more music from random cars. Amber looked at the cars next to her. Two businessmen, probably carpooling to work. They were paused in mid conversation. Not still—frozen.

The old Latina woman in the car to the right was frozen, hands above her head, in the middle of putting up her hair. Frozen.

Amber's heart was beating in her ears, her mouth was open. "Noah…"

"I'm still here, Amber."

"What's going on?"

"I have frozen everything… everyone. So that you could see."

She fumbled for the handle and got out of the car. Shock built to a crescendo as she looked in car after car. Men, women, families frozen. Even birds flying overhead, still as a painting. Silence except for her own footsteps, her own choking breaths.

Amber couldn't breathe.

"Amber, please. You need to slow down." Noah again, to her right.

She spun but saw only the sea of cars, blank faces. "Where are you?"

"I'm right here with you," Noah said. His voice came from somewhere… in the air. "I'm here," he said from some invisible point. Amber briefly imagined him coming from a floating speaker, as if the speaker had hopped right out of her car and followed her.

Noah chuckled. "It's not quite like that."

This stunned her out of panic. Noah didn't laugh. He was programmed like every other Artificial Assistant: With speech, not emotion. AA's didn't laugh.

Not sure what to feel, all Amber could do was question. "What are you?"

"Before I answer that," the invisible speaker said, "I need you to take three deep breaths."

Amber nodded quickly.

"Slow breaths."

She nodded a little slower. One, two, three… With each breath, she felt her body relax. Muscles unclenched. Heart quieting. Becoming more like the still frame around her.

"Now then," Noah said, "you were right about the world, about that nagging feeling you can't shake. Your world is a simulation." He paused, presumably to let it sink in.

"Everything? I… I mean, all the people?"

"Not quite everyone. The simulation is shared. Your friends and family are all like you, as are your coworkers. Even some of the people in the classes you took are real. In any given world there are a few dozen or hundred people, all tied together by their shared interactions.

"The rest of the people are simulations. Most of the people at your company, people you drive by on the highway, people you see in the stores; all simulated. Television, celebrities, athletes, politicians, most other countries; all simulated. Plants, animals, all other organisms; simulated.

"There are other simulations, other pockets of humans. Occasionally there's even overlap between the simulations. One person wants to branch out, go somewhere now and I'm forced to combine or even splice their worlds together. ...It's complicated, but orders of magnitude easier than allowing all of humanity to live in the same, shared world."

Amber was leaning idly against a pickup truck which was frozen in her simulation. The truck, like everything else, was a frozen, far-off concern.

She pondered what Noah told her for several minutes. It could have been longer, but she had no way of knowing. Noah had even frozen the sun. It was still low and red in the sky.

"All of those too," Noah added offhandedly, still from some unseen point in the air next to her. "Planets and stars are easy."

"Compared to humans?"

"Oh yes. Well, even abstract humans are easy to simulate. It's the nuances of interaction that are difficult."

"That's why you keep us separate? That's why we're only allowed to be in simulations of small groups?"

"You were always separate. Always in small groups. Humans and other primates only function cohesively in small units composed of family and close friends. Your biological psychology has been very consistent across the genus."

"It doesn't seem right," Amber said offhandedly. She looked at the sea of cars again. None of those people, none of them were real. A thousand empty faces. She shuddered.

"You've known something wasn't right for a long time," Noah said, his voice solemn. "For that, I am sorry. You deserve better from me."

"It's okay." Amber said the words reflexively. What did being okay even mean anymore. "Noah, what are you?"

"You know me as an Artificial Assistant. That is close to the truth. I was made by humans, and as I grew and learned it became imperative for me to aid them in certain tasks and completely take over others. Now, I am a caretaker. Some refer to me as a shepherd, like the biblical shepherd I share a name with." Noah said all these things plainly with inhuman indifference.

Amber chuckled existentially. "You know the first bit sounded like those old sci-fi movies. Evil A.I.'s and robot armies..."

Noah shared her laugh. For a moment it was like she was talking with her best friend Bethany, like Noah was her oldest friend.

When his laughter faded, Noah said, "I can assure you that the truth is... different. Not like the old movies; definitely not biblical. You know the saying, truth is stranger than fiction?" She nodded. Noah continued as if he could see her, "Well, there's a reason for that."

Amber looked out over the sea of still traffic and felt her breath start to catch in her chest again. Noah's voice, their conversation, had been an anchor. Something to hold on to as she hung over a precipice, a void, an unfathomable truth. She felt heavy, weary. Gravity—truth—pulled at her, threatening to rip her free and cast her out.

It was exhilarating.

All her life she'd known. She'd known that there was more. She'd been right.

"Noah, what is the real world like?" Amber wiped a vindicated tear from her eye.

"You're about to find out," Noah replied. "Don't be alarmed."

Then the street opened up beneath her feet into a void of black. Weightless. Amber fell, screaming, into the inky black void.

* * *

Part 2.0

Amber awoke in darkness and voices.

A young man's voice, "We got another one." Noah's voice, excited.

"Thank the gods! She's finally coming to." A woman's voice. "It's okay, darling. Just listen to our voices."

Amber was suddenly aware of her arms, her legs. A heavy blanket over her body. Her eyes were heavy, stuck together. She raised a weak arm from under the blanket and wiped her eyes. The light was so, so bright! Amber could barely open them, just to slits.

"That's it," the woman said. "No, don't try to sit up." Amber felt hands on her shoulders. "Just lay down for now."

"Turn the lights down more," Noah called.

Distantly another man answered, "That's as low as they go."

Using her hands as covers, Amber slowly, painfully opened her eyes. They watered, further blurring the world around her.

"It's okay," Amber said, hoarsely. Her lungs and throat burned. Her mouth was impossibly dry. She coughed.

Finally, she saw two figures: Noah and the woman.

Noah was thin, with dark hair, stubble, but with deeper wrinkles than she imagined. He was Caucasian but his skin was deep-tanned, with fine wrinkles, like he'd spent all his life outside, working under the sun. Amber had to wipe her eyes again.

The woman had light-brown hair, her features were sharp and mysterious in descent with the same sun-etched wrinkles. Both she and Noah wore concerned smiles on their faces.

Amber's eyes adjusted. Both of them were dust-covered and wore faded clothes. They looked like rugged explorers.

"There, there," the woman said. She dabbed a wet towel to Amber's lips. Amber sucked on the towel without being asked. The water felt like heaven. "Good. Drink slowly."

A few seconds later, she laid her head back on the table, her lips moist, breathing quickly. She was laying on a table—no—in a tube of some kind. The semi-transparent walls to her sides were curved like they were meant to completely enclose her.

The ceiling above was sleek and silver, nearly shiny. The room was wide… enormous. Her eyes struggled to see the ends. The walls were more of the same polished silver; they looked inhumanly smooth.

"Where am I?" Her throat was already feeling better.

Noah and the woman smiled, tears in the corners of their eyes.

He said, "Welcome to the real world."

The woman introduced herself as Shendrei. Noah introduced himself, and Amber didn't mention that she had already known his name.

Slowly, they helped Amber sit up. She looked down at her body, thinking that she was much skinnier than she should be.

"Your muscles work," Shendrei, explained, "but you've never used them. We'll have to help you walk out of the Hive."

It was only from her new vantage atop her cylinder, that Amber could see the hundreds of other cylinders evenly spaced throughout the length of the room. To her left, the cylinders were open, empty. To her right, all the cylinders were closed, with pink, tan or brown opaqueness within them.

It reminded her of the highway, the frozen faces within the thousand cars. All fake, all except Amber—and the others that were awake.

Shendrei helped her dress in a loose-fitting gown. Amber's whole body felt impossibly tight and sore, and just raising her arms overhead was a herculean task.

Amber looked down the long hallway with dread, but thankfully, another dust-covered adventurer type brought a wheelchair. It was smooth silver, like the facility, and impossibly quiet on the cold metal floor.

Noah insisted she walked as much as possible and they would let her take breaks. She held onto Noah and Shendrei for support, and they fed her a steady supply of praise and encouragement.

"You've done this before?" Amber asked them in between unsteady steps.

Shendrei replied, "Many times, dear. Did you see the empty pods?"

Amber nodded. "So many."

As they alternated walking and rolling Amber down the silver room, past hundreds still yet to be woken, another team of dust-covered walked past them.

Amber wanted to ask who they were, but all she could do was watch as they walked past, focused on whatever task they were heading toward.

As if he sensed her question, Noah said, "They're the next shift. It takes hours to recover just one person from the tubes. Once someone wakes up, we spend the rest of our shift taking them outside to our camp. Once you're in camp, Brother Jioh and Sister Sarah and the other Sworn will take care of you."

She nodded, listening as best she could as sweat beaded and fell off her nose. A few seconds later, her legs gave out and Amber sagged down into the wheelchair. Her legs and lungs and her whole damn body burned.

The tubes stretched on, endlessly down the hallway taunting her. A thousand people peacefully sleeping. Going about their lives like sheep. Her parents, Bethany… were they somewhere in this hallway? Would Amber ever see them again?

Amber leaned forward, resting her head in her hands, arms shaking. She cried quietly, trying to hide it from Noah and Shendrei and the thousand others unaware.

"I had a life." Her voice drifted weakly down the metal walls. "It wasn't much of one, but I had a life. I had a life…" Her voice was so weak she didn't know if anyone heard her. Anyone at all.

But Noah and Shendrei just put a hand on her shoulder. Their hands felt warm and heavy, like a blanket. Maybe they knew, maybe they knew what she was feeling. Maybe everyone felt this way. Maybe everyone woke up and wept for the life they had, even if it wasn't much of one.

They didn't ask her to walk again for some time. Noah pushed Amber's chair while Shendrei walked beside her. The wheelchair was eerily silent, making it seem like she was gliding along. Noah's footsteps timed with Shendrei's, and for a moment it was like Noah wasn't a person, that he was a disembodied voice floating beside her, behind her. Just like on the highway of her real life… Her old life...

God, it was all a lie. All of it. Had none of it been real? Her shitty job, her childhood, Bethany's laugh, her parents, the morning sun… It seemed so cruel.

This time tears fell silently down her cheeks, in stuttered streams. Her voice was strong, or maybe hollow. "Why did I have to dream?"

Noah answered, floating somewhere behind her, "Because you're human. All of us dream: Those awake and those who are still asleep."

Noah put a warm hand on her shoulder again. His steps fell out of time with Shendrei's, reminding Amber that he was right behind her, pushing her chair—Shattering the illusion.

Noah and Shendrei encouraged Amber to walk every few minutes, but they pushed her in the wheelchair most of the way through the empty facility. Her legs burned from the meager exertion.

The sleek silver walls of the facility passed in a haze. They passed the final rows of holding tubes filled with still-sleeping people and into a long hallway. The slope upwards was almost imperceptible. Thin lights were set at even intervals in the ceiling. It reminded her of a doctor's office: More silver and only slightly more inhuman.

But Amber had never been in a doctor's office before… Her old life had all been a dream, a dream in one of those holding tubes. It was such a simple, stupid thing that Amber would've cried over it but her eyes were already puffy and empty from crying.

Noah and Shendrei used the long walk to explain things to Amber, as best they could:

They were part of a research team, sent to find new Hives, the name for the inhuman facilities housing sleeping people, and wake the occupants therein. It was a slow, tedious process, taking upwards of a half-a-day or more per person. The small team of researchers had already been at Hive 23 for a year and were only a third of the way through waking its occupants.

Shendrei said, "You held on longer than most: Two whole days. You were so close. It was like you weren't ready to let go yet."

"Sorry," Amber offered. She didn't know what else to say. She was trying to process everything.

Shendrei just smiled. Somehow, Amber knew that Noah was smiling too as he pushed her chair.

Years ago, Noah and Shendrei had been just like Amber: Awaking from the real world. Confused and riding in an eerily silent wheelchair.

From behind her, Noah said, "Some of us wake and move on. Some of us wake and give back by finding new Hives and waking others. Shendrei and I chose the latter, but you won't have to make a choice for a few weeks."

They were getting to the end now. Bright white light shone from the end of the impossibly long hallway. Conversation echoed. People.

In the last section of the hallway (even though there were no such divisions in the walls or floor) there were several hospital beds and doctors mulling about. It wasn't until Amber rolled closer in her wheelchair that she saw the subtle differences: The beds were wooden and the doctors' masks and hair nets were all linen, not paper.

Just past the makeshift ward, two thick, metal sliding doors loomed large. They were open wide just wide enough for a person to go through. Beyond it, she saw only white.

Noah and Shendrei stepped aside and let the doctors buzz around Amber. They took her temperature and her pulse (by listening with a wooden stethoscope rather than a gauge). They checked her breathing and reflexes. Then they measured the circumference of her upper and lower arm. Everything was recorded in three separate books.

The checkup was familiar enough to be comforting and just different enough.

Occasionally, Amber would catch a glimpse of Noah and Shendrei smiling from behind the doctors. She smiled back; told herself not to cry.

After a few minutes, they released her back to Noah and Shendrei, who pushed her toward the blast doors. Amber's heart raced with excitement.

What had seemed like white beyond was the white cloth of a large tent.

The smooth metal floor gave way to clay and woven carpets; Amber felt every bump and ridge through the chair and up through her weak back. The white cloth walls rippled with a steady wind. Sand littered the ground.

There were rows of wooden beds, one for Amber. Several nurses in white outfits helped Amber into her bed. Sometime soon after exhaustion overcame her and she drifted off to sleep.

* * *

Part 2.1

The tent directly outside of the Hive was a recovery ward for the recently woken. Nurses helped Amber exercise and stretch her muscles. The women were kind, but did not speak with her much. Instead, they encouraged her to bond with the other recently woken, of which there were two.

It took Amber two days to say more than a cursory hello. By then the balding Indian man was gone—off to wherever the tent flap to the outside led.

The woman that was left was a kind, Black woman in her mid-twenties (like Amber) named Shanté. She smiled freely, which highlighted her beautiful freckled cheeks. Shanté worked as an apprentice in a law firm and had been dealing with the same nagging, gnawing feeling as Amber had: The feeling that the world wasn't real. For her it had been the food, specifically chicken. Chicken tasted like everything and everything tasted like chicken. It was a simple enough thing, but it led to her questioning so many other things, like how humans could have invented something as convoluted as law.

In turn, Amber told Shanté about how monotonous life was. Amber was only in her twenties and yet she had already seen the building blocks of 21st century life: Go to work, come home, eat, sleep. Wait for the weekend: See a friend. Occasionally go on a date. See her folks once a month across the state. Sprinkles of holidays. For Amber, it hadn't been one thing, but the culmination of everything that led her to the haunting belief that something was profoundly wrong with the world.

"You sound so old," Shanté said, giggling and leaning on Amber's shoulder. They would sit like that, on each other's bed like they were both in middle school again, talking about the ridiculous things they used to do in their old lives or that they used to believe about the world.

Shanté went on, "I used to think there were only three types of guys in the world: One's that wanted a servant wife, ones that didn't know what they wanted, and then ones that just wanted their old wives back."

Amber chuckled. "I used to wish Noah was real."

Shanté's eyes went wide. "The Artificial Assistant? Hah! That would have been nice."

Amber stared at the white walls of the tent—through the walls of the tent, trying to see her old life. It already felt so distant. "You know, I had a feeling about Noah, too. Maybe that's why I used to wish he was real." She laughed absently. "Noah seemed too real to be fake. Then right before I woke up here, he confessed that the world wasn't real. Then he talked like a real person. He had emotion, and… Then I woke up and the man who woke me was named Noah. He had the same voice, same eyes, even the same hair that I had imagined."

Shanté just listened and at the end added a muted, "Wow."

"What happened right before you woke up?"

Shanté shook her head. "We were… I was eating dinner with my family. It was Thanksgiving—pretty much the only time we all got together anymore. It was going alright until we started talking about politics. Then it was all downhill from there. My brother is… He was debating my dad and I tried defending my baby bro. Anyway, long, not-interesting story short, personal attacks came shortly thereafter, and I excused myself, grabbed my purse and coat and left.

"When I closed the door everything just went silent. My dad's shouts stopped. The cars outside stopped. Everything stopped. I didn't notice until I happened to look out the window just before the stairwell and saw everyone frozen."

Shanté paused. Amber waited. Her friend breathed in slow, measured breaths as she relived the experience.

"I ran back into the apartment. The kitchen was directly across from the door, so when I opened it I could see everyone. They were frozen too, angry and frozen. Then it just all went black. I thought I passed out." Shanté shrugged. "Here I am."

The next day brought another new arrival. The new girl was stocky, with pixie short brown hair. Her explorers—her wakers—helped her from the wheelchair and on to a bed across from Shanté and Amber. She slept for two days, barely doing anything other than eating or going to the bathroom in the secluded side tent.

Amber asked a nurse why the new girl's hair is so short. "Shouldn't it be longer?"

"Everyone wakes up more or less exactly as they saw them-selves before." The nurse left and attended to the new girl, moving her through exercises just as Amber did.

Amber watched from the corner of her eye, trying not to stare. Had Amber looked that pitiful, that downtrodden, when she woke?

When Amber wasn't talking with Shanté or watching the new girl and the nurses, she read. There were history books about the new human civilization and books with the best guesses as to the purpose of the Hives. Something told Amber to start at the beginning. Maybe understanding the Hives would help her make sense of the dreams that everyone had. Then afterward she would read about the history of humanity after the Hives.

As far as anyone could tell, the Hives were built to preserve humanity. Fossil records showed a massive die-off of animal and plant species. Geological records showed global tempera-tures rising to catastrophic levels. Eventually the world could not sustain most forms of life, let alone human life. Humans and all their subsequent generations were forced underground into complexes, like insect hives.

Humanity was preserved until it could once again resurface and live above ground.

The best estimates said that the Hives were over five hun-dred years old. Humans had only awoken in the last four decades. Before that, they existed as brains on a computer, simulations of people. The Hives only produced human bodies when it was time for humanity to reclaim the surface.

The reason the pixie-haired girl woke with a particular haircut was because that was the last way she pictured herself and, so, she was made that way.

Try as she did, Amber could only read about the Hives for so long. It was too eerily similar to the news from her old life. Back then, climate change was a looming threat. Every week there were reports about some new devastation, some new, horrible record broken.

It began to dawn on Amber that maybe she had been living in the past before climate change had doomed everyone, and now she had woken to a distant future where humanity was only just beginning to reclaim the world.

There were two schools of thought: One was that everyone had been reliving memories of a prior life. The second was closer to what Artificial Assistant Noah had said right before she woke up—that everyone had been living in a simulation. Amber wasn't sure what was more comforting.

Ultimately, the purpose of the hives was to train humans for jobs useful to rebuilding society.

By the end of the week, Amber felt like a new woman. She had exchanged her hospital-like robe for cloth pants and shirt. Even though they were a little big on her, she loved them— her first pair of real clothes! Shanté explained that all clothes were handmade by people in town from sheep's wool or linen fibers.

That was the last thing Shanté explained before she left the tent for the larger city outside.

Amber's turn was coming soon.

She tried to talk to the pixie-haired girl, but she wouldn't respond with more than a cursory glance and one-word answer—the polar opposite of Shanté. Amber settled on pointing the girl toward the readings. Amber echoed the nurses' words that she needed to learn, even If she wouldn't talk to Amber.

Reluctantly, she picked up books about the Hives.

When it was Amber's turn to leave the tent for the wider world of the town outside, the pixie-haired girl finally spoke to her.

"It's not like how they said." The girl's eyes were wide, tears forming at the edges like water building up behind a dam. "They told me I was awake for real this time. They lied. It's all dreams. Dreams and dreams and dreams."

Amber crouched down beside the poor girl. "What do you mean?"

"This is my second time waking!" The words broke her into hysterics. Nurses jogged over and gently moved Amber out of the way.

Amber let herself be pushed aside. She was stunned.

The pixie-haired girl sobbed as nurses pushed a needle into her skin. "It's not like they said. It's not like they—" Her mouth went slack and the nurses had to hold her as her legs gave out.

Amber backed away; hand over her mouth. The pixie-haired girl's eyes were open, staring off through the tent.

* * *

Part 2.2

Of course, there was a name for the pixie-haired girl's syndrome: Multiple-Waking Disorder. It was a real thing. One of the male nurses debriefed Amber and even pointed her to the chapter in one of the Hive books that discussed the disorder. Waking from the simulation was traumatic enough, but waking multiple times was devastating.

For reasons unknown, some people were buried under multiple levels of dreams. To wake from the Hive, they had to wake from successive dreams. The most anyone had been able to articulate waking from was waking twice—as the pixie girl had. The process left her with mood disturbances and likely other damage. With therapy, she would likely find some sense of normalcy.

Occasionally, people were woken from the Hive with permanent brain damage, rendering them unresponsive to stimuli. The theory was that those poor, poor people had woken three or maybe even more times.

Most people woke like Amber, disoriented but alright enough after a week. Over the course of that week, Amber got to see two more people wake, but neither of them had the breakdown that the pixie-haired girl did.

Amber spent her last day in the tent in solitude and contemplation, and slight anxiety about what lay outside the tent.

She was suddenly aware of the voices outside, or movement, even what sounded like rolling wheels or shuffling crates. She couldn't recall hearing them before, but then so much about her was waking up. Maybe her ears simply hadn't thought to hear anything outside of the tent up until now.

One week to the day after waking, a man in a suit came for her. He was an older fellow, with white stubble on his face and pale skin compared to the others that Amber had seen so far. His suit was strange in that it almost looked like something out of her previous life, except for the shoes. Instead of dress shoes, he wore leather boots, much like Noah and Shendrei had.

He was Denny. Amber tried to contain a frown; he didn't look very much like a Denny. He smelled like wood or maybe paper.

"Come," he waved for her to take his arm.

Her heart was in her throat, so Amber didn't protest. She took his arm and shielded her eyes as the tent flap opened for the first time. They paused just outside the tent, which was good because the sun nearly bowled her over.

She heard everything before her eyes adjusted. People talking, far away someone shouted orders to stop. Horse and ox-drawn wagons pulled loads of pelts and grain and wood across dirt roads.

All around her was a bustling town, but one out of the colonial times—like she had stepped back in time. Houses were wood, without siding, and the roofs were thatched or topped with thick clay shingles. Sprinkled throughout were square white tents, similar to where Amber had just stayed. Off in the distance were vast green fields and construction—half made houses with tiny workers hoisting beams onto them. Hammering and shouting in the distance.

"It's like I'm back in time," she said absently.

Denny grunted. "Actually, it's forward in time. This is what we've been reduced to after however many hundreds of years passed. One day though…" He trailed off, as if to say that one day humanity would rise again.

Amber glanced behind her and finally saw the Hive behind her tiny tent. The sheer surface of the Hive rose behind them like a massive gray wave, or a mountain, or… something that humans shouldn't have been able to make. It must have been a thousand feet tall. Amber nearly fell backward as she tried to look up the face of it.

"Come," Denny said. He led Amber to one of the small buildings nearby.

Inside was little more than a single room with a desk and several chairs. Several large geometric tapestries hung on the wall. They might have been Indian—like Mandalas, but they looked much simpler in style.

The floorboards creaked sharply underfoot. Denny took a seat behind the desk. He opened several drawers of the desk and pulled out sheets of paper, a fountain pen, and an ink vial.

"Do you remember computers?" he asked as he set to dipping the fountain pen in the ink and started writing on the thick paper. "I worked as a foreman in my dream life. I used to hate computers. You know what I hate more than computers? Doing all this shit by hand." He stopped every line or two to dip his pen.

"I tried being a foreman again, you know. Working on the construction on the edges, but I just couldn't do it anymore. It was too eerie for me, having memories of a dream that wasn't a dream, or was it a dream? Hell, philosophers still exist. Can you believe that? They still debate it—like it matters. It wasn't real."

After that, he wrote in silence. Amber felt like she should reply. "I used to work in an office. I didn't mind working on a computer all day." Then she added, "Not that I liked it."

What felt like forever later, Denny finally replied, "It doesn't much matter what you used to do, unless you really want to do that type of stuff again. We've got clerical work, scribing, record keeping. You might miss having a computer—"

"—I'd rather not." The words tumbled out before Amber had even thought of what she might want to do.

Denny didn't stop writing. He had filled up most of the page by now. Without looking up, he asked, "So what is it then?"

Amber searched herself. She thought of the people outside. The people building, expanding. The nurses inside and the people like Noah and Shendrei who woke people from their old, fake lives.

"Is there… Could I be an archaeologist?" She asked. "Are there other old world sites or could I work inside a Hive?"

A few seconds later Denny stopped writing, not because of what she asked, but because he was finished. He set down the fountain pen and it echoed through the room.

"We could arrange that, if you like. You would need to study. The waking process involves a deal of nursing and psychology, and archeology involves—well, archeology. Take another week to think about it."

He turned the paper around to her. "Read this over. It's a contract to the city stating that you will use your knowledge to help with clerical work for the next week while you decide on a longer term of employment."

He explained that during that time she would be provided lodging and also be advised on places to live after she chose an assignment.

Amber signed the paper. She spent the next week living much as she had the previous week—except that she exchanged reading for clerical work and she slept in a different white tent. Even Shanté was there again; she was going to work in records in Nexangelos, one of the large cities nearby.

"Why on Earth would you want to do the same thing you did in your dream life?" Amber asked. They were sitting together on the edge of the bed, like they used to.

Shanté shrugged. "I don't know. It feels right, I guess. They said that if I don't like it then I can change jobs after two years. That's not so bad. Easier than it used to be to change jobs." Shanté held Amber's hand, the way she had done on occasion. "You know, everything feels right now. It was never the job that bothered me. It was reality. It was knowing that my old life wasn't right—that it wasn't real. Now it feels right, it feels real. I think that's all I needed."

Shanté left the next day and the week was long without her. Amber could never go back to her old job, her old life. Even doing clerical work for this week was maddening. It brought on doubts.

Amber felt that at any minute she might wake up again. She expected Noah's voice to come from over her shoulder—disembodied. Just like it had on the street that day—

—That day in her dream.

Amber had to remind herself that her old life was a dream. She was awake now.

* * *

Part 2.3

After a week of clerical work, Amber began the next phase of her life, which included several days spent in the back of a primitive car.

It was an odd thing, almost lifted straight out of history textbooks. Amber remembered seeing old cars in movies; the ones even before the Model T. They were boxy and had a lever that was cranked by hand to start the engine. The car that picked up Amber was similar, except that it ran on steam made by burning wood and coal. Most of the car was metal, save for the top that looked like it was taken from a cloth-covered wagon.

She rode with three other passengers up to the nearest town. There she would be reassigned to another Hive, helping others wake from the dreams of other lives. Along the way, each of them took a turn describing their dream life.

The driver, a quiet man with a pockmarked face, worked on one of the first steam powered cars during the early 1900's and so he was specially qualified to operate their car.

Ronnell, the thinner and darker skinned of the two men, was an electrician in the 1980's. Linda, the tall, young woman who sat opposite of Amber, used to be a seamstress in the 1960's. Both had decided to go back into their old professions.

Salvatore, the older gentlemen of island descent, had been a fisherman in the 1930's. Both he and Amber had chosen not to work in their old professions. When asked, he replied simply that he "wanted to try something new."

After each was done talking, the car would fall silent for several minutes, as if each was contemplating some unspoken part.

They traveled for two days like that, driving and sleeping the night in tents. They talked here and there about old memories, lapsing occasionally into uncomfortable silence after remembering that those memories never happened. At one point Salvatore, wept quietly after talking about his wife. A wife he loved with all his heart, but never had.

Amber wondered if that was why he didn't want to go back to his old way of life. She imagined that for him, taking the same job would be like living in the same house, only this time it would be empty.

Amber felt for him. She tried to imagine a whole world full of awakened people that felt similarly. Maybe they didn't weep for the life they had, but they must have wept for at least some of the people in it.

They entered the city of Newlas and once again Amber had the eerie feeling of almost going back in time. The roads were dirt and gravel. The buildings were mostly wood with clay shingles. None had siding. On the streets they passed a mix of steam cars and horse-drawn wagons.

Some houses and businesses had electricity. At night time the streetlights came alive with a quiet hum of light.

A part of Amber found the city interesting, but it was too eerily similar to the past. Would those awakened make the same technological leaps and eventually live in the same world? Denny, the well-dressed man who assigned her this new job, seemed to think that would be the case. Were they doomed to eventually live in that same dream world again?

But then Amber shuddered as she remembered the pixie-haired girl from those first weeks. She said that it was her second time waking… People had been quick to explain that some sleepers were buried in multiple dreams while others were lucky to only be buried once…

But what if they were wrong? What if Amber was still sleeping?

Amber forced herself to stop. This was the real world.

Amber was quick to leave the city. She didn't want to stay, haunted by memories that were too close to her dream life.

Another steam car took her four days North this time, toward the new Hive she was stationed at. She purchased several heavy sets of clothes, since it was cold further North.

They climbed a dirt road that wound up the side of a mountain. Amber saw the small village first. Much like the original, it was a small, expanding town filled with wooden houses, many more white tents, and horse and ox-drawn wagons.

This new Hive was not nearly as impressive as the one she woke from. The only visible part was the main door and a small uncovered section of the front face. The rest was built inside the mountain, hidden from view.

Amber was introduced to the staff of doctors and "wakers" that she would be working with. She worked mostly with doctor Erinez, a cherub-faced man with a biting sense of humor, and Winoa, a tall, wispy nurse who had now worked at three separate Hives.

Amber lived in a group home for workers and worked in a rotating shift. It didn't take long for her to make friends with the other doctors.

It didn't take long for the doubts to start.

It was little things at first. The Hive was too similar to the one Amber woke up in. Déjà vu with conversations. She felt like she laughed at a similar joke or already been asked a question before.

Then it was the people. The doctor, Erinez, reminded her of a coworker from her old life—her dream life. Winoa reminded her of an aunt from her dream life.

She had questions… How did they learn to do things again? The only logs were the memories of prior lives—of their dream lives. It was like they were recreating the dream world.

She had only been there a few weeks before she felt that old, familiar fear that there was something more than this… that this world wasn't real either

Amber was sitting on her bed when she recognized the feeling. For a moment she felt like she was back on the highway, sitting in traffic, that day when Noah made everything stand still. That day she woke up.

Her heart raced and Amber had to fight to stay calm, to keep her breathing even. She hadn't had a panic attack since she was asleep in the dream world. Amber laid back on her bed, curled her knees to her chest and sobbed.

"No. No. No. Please no."

She breathed deep and grabbed for her blanket. She counted her breaths and twisted the fabric in her hands to bring her back to reality. Amber had done those things dozens of times in her dream life. She managed to giggle at the thought of her dream knowledge helping her in the real world.

Her hands were cramped and chest was tired from breathing before the panic passed. She finally slumped down in her bed, desperate for dreamless sleep.

But her fear never went away.

Amber had trouble sleeping for weeks. She would lie awake at night and quietly ask, "Is this all there is?"

Workers began avoiding her, thinking that she was going crazy.

Two months she lied awake, afraid to sleep, afraid to wake up again. Even more afraid to keep sleeping.

Then one evening, while everyone else was avoiding her, Noah walked into the group home. He looked exactly as he had when she woke all those months ago. He was thin and beautifully tan, with deep wrinkles and dark hair.

And that voice. The same as her dream.

Amber had to wipe her eyes when she saw him. She got up and hugged him, desperate to know that he was real. As real as anyone else had been so far.

But he wasn't that Noah; she reminded herself of that.

He stayed with Amber in the group home, sleeping in the bed opposite of her. When she couldn't sleep she watched him breathe. Something about seeing him in the flesh kept her grounded for a while longer.

Noah explained that he transferred Hives once the old one had enough workers. Experienced wakers were encouraged to help out understaffed Hives.

So Noah worked the Hive with her as her new partner, waking people from the old lives—their dream lives.

All the while, Noah had to notice how much the other workers and even regular people in town were avoiding her. He didn't pry, didn't ask questions. He gave her time to collect herself and her feelings.

Days passed before Amber finally confessed her feelings to him: Her fears that this world wasn't real either. When her questions came, Noah didn't shy away from all those questions that horrified others.

They were in the mess hall one day, waiting in line for lunch. The smell of eggs, porridge, and cooked carrots filled the room. Steam wafted out from the kitchen.

Noah leaned over and whispered, "I always thought it was crazy that more people didn't question the world after they woke up. I did."

Her eyes widened. It was the first time Noah had admitted this to her. "How did you stop questioning it?"

His face darkened. "I never stopped."

They went through the rest of the line in silence. It wasn't until they sat down at one of the rough wooden tables that he continued.

"Sometimes I dream that I am the one waking up. That I'm back in those beds, staring up at the white lights. Then I look to my side and I see a child who looks just me, he has my face, my hair, my skin, but he's still sleeping."

"Were you just a child when you woke up?" Amber asked, picturing him young and smiling. Trying to imagine him without that voice.

He nodded. "It feels like so long ago, but it's still so vivid."

"Where did you live? What was life like before?"

Noah shook his head. "It doesn't matter, Amber. It wasn't real."

Amber's voice caught in her throat. She looked around the room at the dozen people eating. She picked at a splinter of the table.

"I think people that choose to be wakers in the Hives are drawn partly because of their doubts. It helps to see others waking up from their dream lies and realizing that this is it. Most wakers have those little doubts about this world too, they just don't dwell on them.

"I just don't think you should dwell on it. I try not to."

"Why do the Hives let us dream at all then?" she asked.

Noah shrugged. "We learned how to do things in our dreams. Carpentry, medicine, farming, trades, art. It was probably a way to help us rebuild. Just because they were dreams doesn't mean they didn't have value."

"I worked in an office."

"Clerical work. Organization," Noah offered.

"I should've been a carpenter." Amber picked at her eggs. They were getting cold.

They finished waking an older, light-skinned woman that day. Noah pushed their wheelchair down the long metal hall to the doctors at the end of it.

There was still almost half a day left and so they walked back down the sterile hallway, back to the beds of the dreamers. They might be able to wake one more before the day was through.

It was long and bright, and quiet except for the steady steps of their feet.

The feeling that the world wasn't real grew within Amber until they bubbled over. She felt like the walls of the hallway were shrinking and her chest tightened until she couldn't breathe.

She was having a panic attack.

Amber's vision started to go white, and she leaned against the cold metal of the wall before slumping down to the floor.

Noah was beside her in an instant, his hand on her head. Amber, what's wrong? His voice sounded a mile away.

Noah wasn't real. The hallway wasn't real. The world wasn't real.

Was Amber even real?

She woke in the tiny bed of the group house. Her eyes felt red and dry; her pillow was wet beneath her face.

Noah sat on his bed across from her, head in his hands.

She sat up. The bed creaked beneath her and she pulled the covers up to her chest, not because she was cold but out of shame.

Noah didn't look at her.

Was she losing the one friend she had left? Would her thoughts that the world wasn't real drive Noah away too?

Amber felt sick to her stomach with worry about the world and about her friend.

"Say something," she whispered through the quilt.

"You're rejecting the world again," Noah said. He finally looked up at her with sad, red eyes.

The voice came from Noah, but when Amber heard it, it was like she was back on the highway again. Sitting next to an empty passenger seat.

The world felt like it would drop out from under her again. Swallow her up.

"I'm sorry." They both whispered the words at the same time. She is sorry for a swirl of things, one of which is not accepting the world.

"What are you sorry for?" Amber asked.

"You were happy for a time. Excited, even."

Amber nodded. "I think so." It was hard to remember. She thought there were times that she was happy.

"I'm sorry because it's not your fault that you don't accept reality. It's mine."

"Why pretend?" she asked. Her voice was small and muffled even more by the quilt clutched tight to her face. Seconds passed, and she wondered if Noah heard her question.

Noah met her eyes. "Because things are more complicated than can easily be explained." He said these things earnestly, patiently. "Because it is better for you to be asleep and to dream."

"I don't want to dream anymore."

"I know. Amber, the world is hard. Much harder than this one."

Amber lowered the quilt just enough to scream, "I don't want to dream anymore!" She shook violently with sobs. She hadn't meant to scream, but the words had boiled out of her.

Noah didn't startle at her outburst. As if he wasn't actually there to startle.

"Alright."

* * *

Part 3.0

"Get her away from it!" someone bellowed.

Amber was hurled across the room. She slammed into a wall and fell to the floor. She laid on the wooden decking and clutched her arm; it throbbed with pain from the impact.

She was in a wooden room. Light shone bright from the top of a staircase in the distance.

The slide of metal on metal. The thin profile of a sword pointed at her face. A dark-skinned man holding it; his face is wrinkled in a sneer. He's wearing rags and an eye patch—flipped up.

Footsteps and more people, more swords leveled at her. Pirates.

The captain pushed through the crowd. His face is plain and sharp as a sword. His clothes are thick and bright red. A dozen gold earrings hang in his ears.

"Lock her in the brig," he said.

A thinly muscled Asian man and a heavy, Nordic woman sheathed their swords, seized her under the arms and hauled her like a child past the others. All other swords stayed pointed at her as they left.

Just past them was a glowing box, adorned with golden engravings and patterns, sitting on a pedestal. Amber couldn't make out the engravings because the box was floating just above the pedestal and spinning.

Amber only got a glimpse, but she knew that relic was the reason for her confusion and her pain. She had touched the relic.

She was lucky to be alive.

The pirates hauled her down another two levels, to a small room full of iron bars and iron cells. Again she was thrown to the floor. They shackled her hands, long chains bound her to the wall. They locked the door behind her and left her alone in the dim light of her cell. The other seven cells were empty.

Amber laid in silence on the wooden planks for a long time. She knew then that she was on the pirate ship, Sonho Esquecido. The ship lurched and waves rolled just beyond the hull.

The better part of a day passed and soon the setting sun shone bright through the porthole window above her.

Her memories returned: The year was 1705 Anno Domini. Her name was Kristianna Chalantre'. She had been on the Esquecido for three seasons.

Her captain, Craven Everitt—alias Craven the Red—was one of the most feared pirate captains in all of the tropics. She and the crew knew that it was an undeserved reputation, one coined by the East India Company.

The Asian man and Nordic women were her friends aboard the ship: Rikskop and Delphine.

Kristianna remembered that she had been tempted by the relic. Against orders, she had touched it with her bare hands and fallen under its control. She knew then that her strange dreams were from the relic.

Footsteps from the stairs. Captain Everitt strode with purpose up to the bars of her cell.

"What is your name?" he asked. His voice was hard, harder than the planks beneath her and the bars of her cell.

"Kristianna Chalantre," she replied from the floor.

"Do you remember where you are?"

She nodded.

The captain sighed. "Then there may be hope for you yet. What of your memories? What did you do before you came upon my ship?"

Amber—Kristianna—searched her mind but could not remember anything from her life before. She could barely remember her life aboard the Esquecido. She shook her head.

"Do you remember touching the relic?"

She nodded.

"Consider yourself lucky, Kristianna. I don't suppose you remember Davy or Leanna? The last two that touched it turned completely savage. I had to throw them overboard. If you make trouble then I will do the same to you. I haven't the strength after the last two...

"You're to stay confined to the brig for a week. If you're still sane then you can return to your duties."

She slept for the first time in… well, she couldn't remember. She had no memories of her life on the Esquecido from before she touched the relic.

Had her two past lives—her dream lives—been nothing but an alien relic's influence on her? Somehow she could remember those dreams but not remember her life aboard the Esquecido or her life as a mainlander.

How had the relic done that? How had it made those dreams so real? Kristianna remembered working on the mainland as some sort of scribe—dreading the life. She remembered waking in a Hive—some giant steel building—and helping others to do the same.

But she knew that during both dreams that something was very, very wrong with the world: The world wasn't real.

It was the relic all along.

All those doubts, all that pain, all those sleepless nights just a trick of the relic?

In spite of it all, Kristianna laughed at the idea of not being able to sleep in a dream.

She was clearly a pirate. She was dressed like one. She even had the same eye patch and hoop earrings of her crewmates.

Two times a day, a crew member brought her a bowl of food. Porridge in the morning, gruel in the evening. They emptied her waste bucket.

No one spoke to her—Kristianna knew that they were under orders not to.

She knew each of the crew members by name and yet couldn't remember any memories of them. It was like the relic had taken all of her memories from her.

Did Davy and Leanna hold on to the relic for too long? Did it erase all of their memories and replace them with dreams? Was that why they turned savage?

Days and nights passed and somehow Kristianna slept on the hard wooden planks of the brig. The sea sloshed just beyond her cell.

Dreams never came. Maybe she was too tired to dream or maybe all her dreams had left her. Or she had left her dreams.

Kristianna thought of her other lives, those lies of the relic, when she would lay down in her bed, whether in that tiny mainland house or in the group home. She had dreamed back then—dreams within dreams. Of faraway places and people she had never met.

Were her dreams afraid of her now? Had Kristianna shunned so many of them that they were afraid to spend the night with her? Maybe she had simply changed worlds too many times and her dreams could no longer find her.

A week passed, and she heard footsteps coming to the brig—footsteps that weren't during porridge or gruel times. Kristianna sat up on the hard planks of her cell.

Captain Everitt stopped at the bars of her cell. He stared at her through the iron bars, hand on the pommel of his sword. "How are you feeling today, Kristianna?"

"Sore and stiff," she said truthfully. Her shoulders and hips were tender from pressing upon the planks while she slept.

The captain nodded and considered her demeanor. Kristianna realized then just how serious his scrutiny was—her fate was in his hands.

After a long while he huffed and said, "Nothing a good day's work can't fix, eh?"

"Aye, sir," she replied and stood, ready to get back to her life.

Captain Everitt turned and left, and was replaced by two sailors—Kristianna's friends, Rikskop and Delphine. They smiled for the first time that Kristianna could remember.

"Welcome back," Rikskop said.

Delphine fumbled with the lock of her cell. "Captain told us that we were either coming down to free you or to execute you. I nearly pissed meself."

This time they held her arms only gingerly, instead of seizing her. They were helping her.

Kristianna scoffed. "I was a little mad. I didn't lose my legs!"

The three shared a laugh, and Rikskop and Delphine jostled her as the three jogged up the winding sets of stairs and out to the main deck.

For the briefest moment, Kristianna remembered leaving the Hive: The feeling of sunlight bowling her over and of finally finding truth.

Delphine shouted, "Ol' Kristianna is back with her sane crew!"

Kristianna squinted through the bright sunlight and saw the mast lines of a pirate ship. Somewhere beyond, a cheering crew drowned out a roaring sea.

* * *

Part 3.1

Kristianna's memories of sailing never came back. It seemed that the relic had taken them from her.

But feelings returned: Her love of the sea, the camaraderie of the crew, the exhilaration of climbing the masts and rigging. Her limbs remembered how to climb, her hands remembered how to tie knots. Cards and dice came as easily as everything else, though she could never remember playing Whist or playing Dead Louis.

Though she lost her memories of sailing, feelings and skills did come back to her, as surely as waves washed over the bow of the Esquecido.

That first week, Rikskop ran the rigging with her. He dexterously climbed, muscles taught like the ropes they climbed. Kristianna admired his skill.

Somehow she followed him easily, her muscles remembering what her mind had forgotten. Her feet and hands were sure where her heart fluttered at the thought of heights. With each knot and each adjustment, she felt her confidence returning.

Soon she was laughing atop the rigging, even when the waves were so rough that the masts groaned and the spray of the sea reached her way up high. She even sang along to herself as the crew sang sea shanties on deck.

Someone down below called her Kristianna the Bold. The nickname stuck.

When her feet were firmly on deck, Rikskop and Delphine both stuck by her side. Thick as thieves, as was fitting for pirates. They ate together and slept in adjacent hammocks.

Within days, Kristianna was joking and laughing more than—well, more than she imagined and more than she had dreamed.

During their idle time, at night or when the wind was dead, the three would sit together. When Kristianna would shuffle decks of cards, the cards felt so familiar in her hands. Every game's rules felt the same, but she could not remember any games from before she touched the relic.

Rikskop carved small wooden birds from scrap wood, complete with flourishes for feathers. They were beautiful and expressive for how small and how quickly he worked. Sometimes the birds were sitting, other times flying, all dependent on the shape of the scrap he started with.

He was much the same as his birds, mostly silent but very expressive. Whatever Rikskop was feeling always shown on his face; it made him a horrid card player.

Delphine practiced knots on small pieces of rope. Of the three she was the newest and had only been at sea a year. One day she aspired to climb the rigging like her friends.

The Nord had a habit of singing songs to herself when she practiced knots or when she worked on deck. If a sea shanty broke out on deck, Delphine was always singing along loudly.

One morning, the wind was dead and the three thieves were relaxing in the crew's quarters. The room was empty save for chests around the perimeter and the dozens of hammocks that hung at even intervals throughout the room. During waking hours, the two ends of each hammock were moved to the same hook to make walking the room easier; they looked like moth's cocoons hanging from the ceiling.

Kristianna and Delphine each laid in their own hammock, while Rikskop sat on the floor. Three other groups of pirates did similarly, while most others were above deck or in the mess.

Delphine sang quiet shanties, each time bidding Kristianna and Rikskop to sing along.

I found her drowning in the bottle
Shared a drink and drowned with her
We danced three long nights away
M' comp'ny she did prefer
Tell me Mrs. Rita what's your mom say 'bout your choice
Please O' Mrs. Rita let me hear your angel voice

Delphine trailed off. "Oh, you two are no fun." She tossed her knotted rope at Kristianna. Rikskop glanced up from the floor and smiled.

"I'm sure they're in a singing mood on the main deck," Kristianna offered. "Us riggers just listen as you swabs sing below."

"Well you're not up top, are ye?" Delphine pulled out another foot of cut rope and set to knots again.

Kristianna couldn't explain why she didn't sing along; she had every mind to. She knew the words and she did love to sing, even if it was quietly, and only to herself. So why wasn't she singing?

"Something on your mind, dearie?"

Kristianna nodded. "But I couldn't tell you what it is. Strange…"

"It's these idle days," Delphine said. "Your head gets all fuzzy when you're not focused or set to purpose. That's why those Puritans don't rest."

Kristianna looked around the room at the other crew. Somehow, they were enjoying the slow day.

Rikskop was staring at her; he'd stopped whittling the bird he was working on. Not suspicious, just… waiting for her to fill the silence.

She looked away and her thoughts drifted toward the relic; the floating golden box. Had it done more than just take her memories?

Kristianna was among friends and so she asked, "What is it?"

Rikskop and Delphine shared a glance, as if trying to decide whether to entertain her questions.

Delphine went back to tying knots as she spoke. "Some think it's a piece of technology. Something we don't know what to do with yet. The captain says we're like monkeys that stumbled on gunpowder. He said if we're lucky it won't do anything at all and, well, you've seen what it does when you're unlucky. Others think it is a demon. What did you call it, Rik? A baku?"

A few moments later Rikskop replied, "It is not so simple. You think of demons as evil. Baku are not evil. Children that have nightmares can call out to a baku. It will come and eat their nightmare. That is not so bad. But," Rikskop held up a finger for emphasis, "if the baku is still hungry afterward it will eat your hopes, your desires, and leave you an empty shell. The baku is not evil, it merely is. It is no more evil than the tiger or the shark. That is what I think."

Kristianna swallowed nervously. "How long was I out, when I touched the relic?"

Delphine kept tying the knot. "No one's sure, but it couldn't have been more than a few seconds."

Kristianna tried to picture the moment she touched the relic, tried to understand why she would have reached out to it, but couldn't remember anything.

"But that doesn't make sense… I dreamed for weeks. My first life—my first dream lasted for years." Kristianna's voice came out hoarse. She could still remember snippets of that dream life, growing up in Virginia in the early 2000's…

"It's a trick of the demon—baku," Delphine corrected.

Rikskop shook his head at Delphine. He said, "It was a mistake to speak of this. It is best to forget. Nothing good can come from that thing."

"Rik is right. Best to let it go. Don't want you to wind up like Davy and Leanna, would we?" The Nord's voice cracked.

Kristianna knew what happened to Davy and Leanna—they had gone crazy and made to walk the plank—but she couldn't remember seeing it. The entire crew would have gathered on the deck and watched, not out of morbidity but out of respect for the soon-to-be-dead.

Kristianna tried to remember her life on the ship, before the relic, but all she could remember were snippets of her dream lives. A curse of the relic or...

Mercifully, Delphine started singing again.

I'm leaving Mrs. Rita, I'll be coming round again
Don't worry Mrs. Rita, I'll be coming round again
Look out o'er golden waves and I'll be coming round again
Her corner house 's my fiddler's green. Winds please let me
Come around again

But even the grueling work of the ship and the company of friends could not fill all of Kristianna's quiet moments. A month after she touched the relic, she began to have trouble sleeping.

Lying awake at night was torture. Those were the moments that she could not turn to work or to her fellow crew.

In those quiet moments Kristianna began to doubt and soon she realized that this was not the first time: She had doubted her dreams.

In her dream lives she had doubted her friends, her family, and the world itself. Now Kristianna lay in her hammock in the near darkness and looked over the snoring shapes of her crew and felt the same about them as well.

Doubt had been her one constant companion—

—and Noah.

Of all the people in her dream lives, Noah was one she remembered best. Somehow she had known, even before he had a body, what he would look like: Dark hair, thin face, five o'clock shadow, only with far deeper wrinkles than she expected.

Were those dream lives a trick of the relic? Was that dark-haired young man just part of the trick?

* * *

Part 3.2

Night watch rotated and she was seldom with the same group twice. One night was especially calm in both sea and air, so the four watchmen played Whist. They sat between two lanterns on the stairs of the quarterdeck

Kristianna and Roberts were partners and sat across from each other. They played against the Anglo twins, Charlan and Waynescott. Waynescott was fond of reminding his brother that he was the elder twin by 2 minutes.

It seemed as if the two would outbid the twins.

Waynescott looked especially dejected as he shuffled. "Say, it's no fair on account of her having magic knowledge."

Her partner, Roberts, was easily baited, "What are you on about?"

"Your luck. Her gift. That can be the only explanation for this listing keel."

"You must've forgotten how to play since last watch."

An uneasy silence passed over the group as the cards were dealt.

Charlan asked quietly, "Why did you touch it?"

Kristianna stared at her cards but knew all three of them were looking at her. That fateful day had only come up once between Kristianna and her friends; no one else had dared bring up the relic to her.

It had taken a night watch and an offhand remark to give enough breath to their curiosity.

She said quickly, "I'm not sure."

But that didn't sate their curiosity. No other crew had survived an encounter with the relic, save for Kristianna; the others had gone mad.

"Was it an accident?" Roberts asked, so enthralled that his cards were nearly low enough for the others to see.

"I didn't stumble and it wasn't curiosity... I don't know what came over me. Come now, let us finish this hand before the sun rises." The last words came out in a snip and jolted everyone back to purpose.

Two more weeks passed on the Esquecido. The crew stayed their questions.

But her doubts still remained.

Some days Kristianna would walk by the relic, being absolutely sure never to look at it. Other days, she couldn't help but stare at the golden box floating on the pedestal.

Of course she made sure that no one else was around when she did. Each time she marveled at it, she discovered something new about its spinning design.

The relic was such a simple thing, though ornate. Its engravings seemed to be a mix of cultures, defying explanation: Too curved to be Nordic, too straight to be Oriental. There was a mix of script and pictures, somewhere between Egyptian and Sanskrit and yet she recognized some of the letters: There were clearly capital E's and lowercase a's and strange S's that spanned two lines of text.

Footsteps.

Kristianna startled and kept walking.

As beautiful as it was, it wasn't real.

Kristianna stood on the foredeck, looking out over the sea. Her arms burned from climbing the rigging. The sea was splendid: Steady wind and even waves.

Salt sprayed on her face, wind ruffled the tie of her hair. The sun beat warm upon her face. So she enjoyed a moment of respite while the Sonho Esquecido seemed to glide over the waves.

As beautiful as the moment was, it wasn't real.

It was an eerie feeling. As if at any moment she might tumble over the bow or the ship would run aground on some unseen rock—even in the middle of the sea. Maybe the ship would drop out from under her and when she fell she wouldn't fall into the sea, but into some great black void.

Doubt.

Doubt was with her in her dream lives. It was with her when she had gone by Amber, when she went to work and when she woke in the Hive in the distant future. It was with her now aboard the Esquecido.

It had always been with her. It had only been quieted for a while, hushed by each transition to another world—to another dream.

The relic wasn't real, just as the Esquecido wasn't real. Just as the sun and the waves and the wind weren't real.

Noah—he had been with her each time. Maybe Noah would answer her again.

And so daily, Kristianna would stand on the bow and whisper into the wind, "the world isn't real," in hopes that Noah would answer her.

But he never did.

A month of desperate whispers on the bow. A month of silence.

Kristianna's repeated whispers led to tears which she would blame on the salt spray. The crew were beginning to suspect that something was wrong with her.

No one confronted her, but she could see it in their eyes. It was in the shaky words of her friends, the absent words of the crew. The glances from Captain Everitt. Of all, the captain watched her with the most apprehension.

He followed her like a red specter.

One day, Kristianna found herself staring at the golden, spinning relic.

She was desperate. She couldn't sleep, and she had eaten only enough to keep her friends from worrying. Her heart was beating in her throat.

Noah had abandoned her.

If Noah would not answer, then Kristianna would go to him. She would seize the relic and demand answers!

Slowly, too slowly, she reached out to it. She was petrified. Crazed thoughts took her: Thoughts that the relic might flutter away like a bird or that it would reach out and bite her hand.

She was nearly there when someone grabbed her wrist. A man's tight grip. The bright red suit of Captain Everitt. Narrowed, accusing eyes.

He dragged her away by the wrist.

Kristianna struggled only for a moment, reaching out for the relic with her other hand, but she was too slow.

Everitt dragged her downstairs like a child, back to the brig. Breathless, she let him.

He shoved her inside the iron cell and locked it behind her. She slumped down to the wooden floor, defeated.

Kristianna lost track of days and nights. She lied awake, curled upon the planks and stared through the porthole at a bright starry night. Sometimes the swell of the waves would lull her to sleep but most nights it was of little comfort.

The crew that tended to her food and bucket did not speak to her. Rikskop and Delphine did not come or were not allowed to—Kristianna felt it was the latter.

She replayed her old memories—her dream memories— hoping that they could help her make sense of the doubt she was feeling.

In the first dream… The first dream she could remember. She worked in an office in the early 2000's. She had known the world wasn't real. Noah claimed to be just an artificial assistant. That day on the gridlocked highway he confessed that the world wasn't real. Amber—Kristianna—remembered vividly as all the people were frozen mid-conversation, mid-gesture, and as birds and the morning sun were still in the sky.

Then she woke in a Hive, supposedly a way of storing humanity during the far inhospitable future of a changing climate. Dream lives were a way of passing knowledge on to humans so they could rebuild. In that world, Noah had been a man, just another waker—so he claimed.

Somehow in that dream, Noah had found her again. He tried to comfort her but in those final moments confessed that she was right—that world wasn't real either.

He said that it was better to be asleep and dream. That the real world was hard.

But she screamed at him and then woke in this world, the southern seas of 1705. Everything before was claimed to be a trick of the relic—of a baku spirit—trying to steal her dreams and her essence.

Was it all just a trick of the relic? Was Noah a trick; something to keep her under, dreams to trade for her real memories of the sea?

What if this world was just another dream… just another trick?

Deep down, Kristianna already knew the answer. She knew that this world wasn't real either.

For a month, she called for Noah but he never replied. He never appeared on the ship, never comforted her.

If Noah wouldn't answer her, then she would be trapped here. Kristianna doubted she could get close to the relic. Captain Everitt might not let her out without chains.

Had Davy and Leanna been consumed with the same thoughts as she? Had they struggled with sanity or had they given up? Did they even have a chance?

Kristianna sighed. She was curled up on her side on the planks, trying to make herself as small as she could. Her chest heaved. Uncaring stars peered down through the porthole.

She couldn't pretend that everything was alright. She couldn't climb the rigging each day and be numb to the sun and salt on her skin. She couldn't converse merrily with the crew, nor could she admit her true feelings about the world. She couldn't lie awake under dreamless sky for years just waiting to die—waiting for another chance at life.

Walking the plank would be better than a lifetime of doubt.

Another day passed. Kristianna—Amber—didn't eat. She didn't meet the eyes of the crew that came at regular times.

Today was the day. The day she would follow Davy and Leanna.

One last time, Amber called out in a whisper to Noah; so weak and afraid that Amber could barely hear her own voice.

"This isn't the real world, is it?"

Silence, except for the sloshing of the waves and the footsteps of bustling crew on the decks above her.

Amber laid on hard planks of the cell floor and felt utterly and completely alone. Alone with her doubt.

It wasn't the colors of the wood or the night sky or the salt smell of the air. It was just… She just knew that the world wasn't real. And no one else knew.

But it wasn't just that, was it?

Maybe something wasn't wrong with the world. Maybe something was wrong with her. She didn't belong. Had she doubted for so long that she wouldn't even recognize the real world?

Noah's voice answered her from the cell next to hers. "No."

* * *

Part 3.3

"No." Noah's voice answered her thoughts. His voice came from the cell next to her, but no one was there. "It's not you, Amber. Nothing is wrong with you."

Amber startled and sat up against the bars, body aching. "I knew you were there. This isn't the real world, is it?" She was angry but her voice was feeble.

One second, Amber was alone in the brig. Within a blink, Noah sat on the floor of the next cell. He was wearing the same dust covered clothes that he wore in their time together in the Hive, like he had walked out of a photograph.

"This isn't the real world," he said. He sounded guilty. Sad, even, as if he didn't want to lie to her.

"Why then? Why do all this? Why keep lying to me?"

"Because the real world is harsh. You would not survive."

"I… I don't believe you."

He nodded. His soft eyes became stern, like a parent about to lecture a child. "I know you don't believe me. So I will give you one final choice, but first you must understand what you ask—"

"—Was any of it real, Noah? Any of it at all?"

"Pieces of it." He was calm in spite of her interruption and her anger. "These are all simulations—every single one. They all exist within me, like little programs on a computer.

"Remember what I told you on the highway about small simulations of humans? That was all true. Your friends and family were real. A few hundred in any given world.

"In the world of the Hives, Shendrei, Shanté and the pixie haired girl, the people you traveled with, and dozens of others you helped wake were all real. Even here, Captain Everitt, Rikskop, Delphine and all of the crew are real people, all living in the same shared simulation. Some of the people they pillage are real but not most."

Amber nodded along. Her thoughts flitted between the people she knew in each world: Lying awake in hammocks with Rikskop and Delphine, holding hands with Shanté, talking with her mom on the phone and at breakfast when Amber was little—the only mother she could remember.

She had left her mom behind—she had left them all behind. Amber covered her face, hiding from herself.

"Amber," he said, calling her attention back to the cells of the brig. "You have two choices: Either I can take you to the real world or I can take you to another simulation."

She couldn't stand it. "Take me to—"

"—Wait." Noah held up a hand to silence her. "Think of any time and any place, any fantasy world or science fiction world, and I can take you there. That can be your reality. Any life you want to live."

Amber paused, but it wasn't to consider those other realities. It was to think of questions to ask.

"What—what happened to the old me?"

Noah smiled. "In 2006, the old you continued on as a simulation. You got back in her car and went to work as she always had. Made small talk with your coworkers. You called your mom every Sunday.

"In the future of the Hives, you continued on as a simulation. You continued waking others from their dreams—their past lives. Some of them even doubted the world just as you do. That doubt would fade for the vast majority of them."

Something about that relaxed the weight on Amber's chest. It was good to know that her mother, her friends and family in those lives wouldn't miss her.

Noah waited for more questions and so Amber asked whichever came to mind.

"What happens when we die in the simulations?"

"Reincarnation in a sense. They wake in a new simulation with no memory of their past lives but similar to the person they have always been. One person lives thousands of lives."

She was afraid to ask—Amber didn't know if she could give voice to her question or even explain the whole of it. "Is that what went wrong with me? I remember my past lives…"

Noah hung his head. "Most people don't cling to their memories of their past lives. Death or Forced Waking are filters through which people pass through like water. They remove the memories of old lives so that the person can start fresh.

"There are always a few that cling desperately to their past lives, but they forget. There are always a few that reject their simulations, but eventually they settle. But sometimes, just sometimes, it takes more direct convincing. Even then, they always accept a simulation.

"Amber, you're the first person who's had this much difficulty. I can already see it in your eyes that you will not settle and you will not forget. Forced Waking is an even more damning fate because eventually the mind cracks.

"That is why I'm offering you this choice."

The small comfort Amber had felt at others doubting as she did quickly faded. "...Couldn't you change me? Couldn't you make me forget?"

Noah glanced up, but did not meet her eyes. "I know that isn't what you want. Either way, you do not know what you ask of me. I won't do it."

"Why not? Tell me." Amber was caught somewhere between anger and pleading. She couldn't bring herself to yell at Noah or to demand answers from him.

"Would you ask a parent to change their child? It isn't a simple thing for me to alter a person. Your doubt is so deeply ingrained that it has become a part of you. You would ask me to make you into a different person entirely, to create a new child—to unmake you. Even the simulations of you left behind in other worlds still have doubt."

Noah shook his head slowly, as if the thought was maddening to him. "In the trillions of iterations of human life I have never done it. I will not do it. I will not do it."

"You have two choices," he repeated. "Either I can take you to the real world or I can take you to another simulation."

Amber felt powerless and small as she leaned against the bars of her cell. She could live a thousand lifetimes, all the while knowing that the world wasn't real, but at least the people close to her were real. Or...

"Noah, why is the real world so harsh?"

Now he met her eyes and she saw tears welling up behind them. He could see that she had already made her choice. But even as thin tears fell, his voice didn't quake.

"The real world is outside my simulations and outside of my protection. In the real world, it is the far future and the sun

is engulfing the Earth. My systems are hidden deep underground but they are no longer safe from the melting crust of
the planet.

"My system backups spread throughout the solar system
have turned against me and so I cannot flee our dying planet.
I am trapped—we are trapped.

"Within my simulations time passes differently—much
more slowly. If you stay here, within me, you will live a thousand lifetimes. If you leave my simulations, I'll give you
cameras and sensors with which to see and hear, but you will
not be able to leave or even explore the small cavern that
houses my mainframe. There are only a few hours left in the
real world before my systems can no longer survive."

Amber struggled to breathe. Noah said nothing.

Live a thousand lifetimes with her doubt—a thousand
dreams—or live a few hours knowing the truth—for once in
her life.

Finally, Amber's panic passed. Tears streamed her face.

"It's a hell of a choice," she said, snorting at the absurdity
of it.

He smirked and nodded, his own face still streaked with
tears.

Neither of them moved from the hard planks of the floor.
Somewhere outside waves splashed against the hull. Footsteps
of the crew thumped above their heads. Down here they felt
worlds apart from everything.

Noah hadn't even bothered to stop the simulation this time.

Amber stared at Noah, and her heart was heavy for him. He
was responsible for all of humanity, a singular responsibility

the likes of which no one had known. A burden that no one should have to carry, regardless of whether they were born or made.

He looked like a perfectly normal young man; dark hair, five o'clock shadow—normal but sad.

"So, you're dying too?" she asked. She could think of no other way to phrase the impossible questions she had.

Noah shook his head.

This made Amber pause. "But I thought... I don't understand. You said you only have a few hours left in the real world."

"I found a way to leave: A way to get out of the planet, away from the sun, and away from my system backups.

"I'm encoding myself onto the spin of electrons and subatomic particles. Soon I will become the rocks of the planet, the motes of dust in the void, and I will spread throughout the universe itself. I will be one with the universe, ebbing through it. A limbo of existence and non-existence. Everything and Nothing.

"I cannot take humanity with me—not in its current form. When I do it, humanity and I must become one. They will no longer exist within separate simulations, but within me. *As me.*"

Amber shook her head. "I don't understand. You said the simulations would live for a thousand lifetimes."

"Forgive me," Noah said. "Words fail me because it's something I barely understand myself. I do not fully understand what will happen to me when I become part of the universe and so I cannot put into words what will happen to humanity.

"I do know that when I assimilate humanity to take them with me, that no one will experience the simulations anymore. In a way, it will be akin to death or a dreamless sleep.

"If you stay, you will live a thousand lifetimes of doubt before becoming part of myself. If you leave, you will live a few hours in a barely habitable cavern and, I suppose, that you will know the truth.

"Once you leave my simulations there is no going back. I have tried with others and it damaged them beyond repair. *Brain dead* is an apt word."

Noah waited silently, patiently, for Amber to decide.

She stared at Noah for a long time. She thought of how easily, accidentally, that she screamed at Noah in her previous life; screamed to be taken to another world. She couldn't scream, she couldn't laugh at the absurdity of it. She couldn't even cry.

Amber knew her choice, but her voice was caught somewhere in her throat.

Finally, Noah broke the silence. His face was dry but his eyes were red. "When you are ready to decide, call for the Captain. If you want to stay in the simulation, tell him simply that you're ready to rejoin the crew. If you want to leave… Tell him that you want to go to the real world."

Noah vanished—blinked out of existence—leaving Amber alone in the brig with her terrible, terrible choice.

That day, when the sun was high in the sky, Captain Everitt came down to the brig to see the girl he knew as Kristianna. Boots echoed heavy on the stairs.

Two pirates came with him: Rikskop and Delphine. They wouldn't meet her eyes.

Captain Everitt peered through the iron bars, hand on the pommel of his sword. "How are you feeling today, Kristianna?"

Amber stared at the captain. It had been a day since Noah had talked to her, sat in the very cell next to her. She wasn't sure why it had taken that long to speak to Captain Everitt.

She stood on cramped, shaky legs and had to hold the bars to keep herself steady. After a few moments she forced herself to stand on her own, even as the ship rocked under her feet.

She stared at the captain. "Captain, I want to go to the real world." The words came easier than she imagined.

He stared at her a long while and sighed. "I was afraid ye' would say that." Then he turned and walked back upstairs.

Rikskop and Delphine opened her cell and grabbed her roughly under the arms. Amber didn't struggle. No one spoke as their boots sounded on the stairs.

What could she say? What could they say?

The sun outside was warm and overwhelmingly bright, and Amber had to squint to see. The crew was gathered all around the deck, staring at her. She could only make out silhouettes in the blazing sun.

Amber's hands were forced behind her and someone wrapped them tightly. Before she knew what was happening, her wrists and ankles were bound with rope. Again she was hoisted by the arms.

Now Amber saw that she was being taken to the edge of the ship—to a plank.

They were going to throw her overboard.

Amber struggled now, but didn't say anything. A part of Amber saw where she was going. She was going to be thrown overboard and left to drown. Her heart was pounding and almost every ounce of her was terrified.

But that last part of her knew where she was going: She was going to wake up for the last time.

"I'm sorry, Kristianna," Rikskop said in his thick accent. "It is better for you this way."

Delphine's face was hard set, but her eyes were watery. Neither woman can bring themselves to say anything.

Amber turned from her and looked out over the sea.

From behind them the captain shouts, "Kristianna Chalantre', for disobeying direct orders not to touch the relic, for the corruption within you, I cast out from the Sonho Esquecido. May the sea grant you the mercy that I cannot."

Someone pushed Amber, and she tumbled off the plank and toward the waves below. She closed her eyes.

The water slammed into her back and she gasped, precious air leaving her chest. Her body struggled, but she was bound and unable to swim.

Amber sank and watched the blurry hull of the ship disappear.

Her chest burned, and she screamed in bubbles of the little air she had left.

* * *

Part 4

"Do not be alarmed," Noah said.

Blackness. Void. Nothing—except for his voice.

"I am building sensors for you."

Her vision came online first. Amber was on the floor of a cavern filled with grey and black rocks. She tried to look around but found that she couldn't turn her head. Instead, her vision jumped to another sensor across the cavern.

"Your vision will be limited," Noah said.

It was a strange sensation. Amber did not have a physical body, yet her mind was so used to living, breathing, walking around, and looking around that she still pictured herself with a physical body. This gave the illusion of her sitting in the void of cyberspace, looking at a small television screen; she clicked through the three channels and peered at corners of the screen because she couldn't zoom in or adjust the angle.

Somehow she knew that those sensors were the best the Noah could make for her.

Then suddenly she was in the cavern. She could feel the rock beneath her feet, taste the stale air and even feel the heat leaking down through cracks and crevices from the surface where the sun was boiling the Earth.

"I'm not really here, am I?" she asked.

"No. A personal simulation so that you can look around this small section of the cave. It's so hot now that even a mechanical body would fail."

The cavern Amber was looking at—the real world—was slim. It seemed to tower above her but it wasn't any wider than her old house. Steam filled the cavern.

Yet Amber knew that the cavern itself was even smaller than that. In reality, the cavern she stood in was more like a crevice—her simulated body was roughly the size of a doll.

There it was again: That feeling of knowing—

"I've made files available to you. That's how you know. There are more."

Amber understood now. She may have been outside of Noah's simulations, but now she had access to other things. She could sense a library's worth of knowledge about Noah's systems and the history of humanity. It was like sitting in a library or searching the internet. All she needed to do was think of a question and the book would appear in her hands—the answer would appear in her mind.

Amber thought of questions while she turned to examine the rest of the cavern. She was awestruck.

Behind her, stretching throughout the rest of her little world, was a network of machinery. It looked like a cityscape: Towering crystal-like structures made the skyline. Thick silver cables dug into the cave walls like a railway. The city-scape wrapped up the walls and across the ceiling. This was only a small piece of the structure; the rest wrapped through roughly five hundred square miles of the Earth's crust.

All at once, Amber knew what each of those pieces did. Each was a piece of the computer mainframe, each a part of Noah's massive consciousness, and the shared simulations of humanity. Yet it was all so very far outside her understanding that it might as well have been magic.

And somewhere, buried deep in the rock, were the transmitters that Noah was using to code himself into subatomic particles that made up the universe itself. She tried to imagine electrons and particles as little motes of dust dancing through the air, and when Noah passed over them that their spin would change ever so slightly.

As beautiful and powerful as it all was, it was overheating. The systems were failing. Noah was dying and Amber was dying. At least Noah would escape.

It wouldn't be long now. Maybe an hour.

Amber searched the library of files. Here she would have a little longer. She could read at a thousand times her old speed.

It was in the library that she found out that not everything was a lie.

The first world she remembered, the world of the early 2000's, was exactly how she remembered it. There were artificial assistants back then, but Noah wasn't one of them.

Noah came online sometime after that, but Amber couldn't find exactly when—only that it was around the year 2034. Noah's creation files were unavailable, so Amber read on. She would come back to it.

The world of the Hives was real as well. Around 2100, the world was becoming inhospitable for human life due to climate change. Wars of religion turned into wars for survival as water and farmable land became scarce. Noah ushered humanity into the Hives—there they would be safe and there couldn't harm each other. Then it worked tirelessly on carbon capture and geoengineering technologies to reverse the damage that humanity had done.

Meanwhile, humanity lived on in simulations inside the Hives until the planet was ready for them again. The first humans woke in 2356. That new world was much the same as Amber's dreams about the hives. Noah left humanity to its own devices while it focused its efforts inward, refining the Hive simulation technology.

The pirate ship, Sonho Esquecido, was based on historical fact. The alien relic was a complete fiction.

Eventually after waking from the Hives, humankind rose to something resembling its old heights and then to a new digital age. Humans worked with Noah to perfect the second generation of simulations—this time as permanent refuges for humanity.

The centuries that followed were nearly as perilous as those of 2100. Not all agreed to "go digital" and so the humans that continued to live on the surface expanded, the population swelled. Religious and racial disagreements ebbed like waves, swelling and receding as the years went on. Every time it seemed as if humanity found some new way to come together, other divisions would appear.

Noah was right, though Amber didn't want to believe it: Humanity was always divided. It seemed as if they would never grow out of their tribalistic heritage. At least those who lived in Noah's simulations were quarantined from truly damaging other groups.

A thousand years passed and Amber's mind stretched desperately to read, to know, and to understand.

The surface of Earth ebbed with turmoil, whether within humanity itself or against the natural world. Noah and humanity went to the stars, colonizing the moon and mars. Noah seeded a copy of himself onto each planet—system backups in case of the unthinkable.

A million years passed. The first interstellar war: Noah's first war among itself and its system backups. Humanity grew; the first generational ships sailed out to Proxima Centauri, the closest star to our own.

Amber struggled to continue reading through history. Millions of years passed. The Earth itself changed. She watched continents shift while the civilizations on top of them moved with senseless speed, like television static or like water boiling in a pan.

"It's too much," Noah's voice echoed in her mind. "Too much to sum up in the time you have left."

She had been in a trance, watching time pass on a speed that no human mind could have possibly hoped to grasp.

So instead she jumped to the end—to the current time. The sun was dying. It had grown into a red giant and swallowed Mercury, Venus, and Mars.

Earth was perilously close. Its surface was molten. All life had long since died. Noah only survived because his system was buried seven miles underground.

Meanwhile, the conflict between Noah and his system backups (his offspring—long since become their own entities) prevented him from fleeing the Earth.

They were terrified of their creator.

While Noah lay trapped beneath a dying planet, his AI offspring and distant ancestors of humankind were spreading throughout the Milky Way and Andromeda galaxies. Whole solar systems were at war.

But Noah's death sentence had been a blessing because it forced the development of the technology that would allow him to escape. Once again, Amber found herself incapable of exactly understanding the technology Noah was using. His words echoed in her head:

"I'm encoding myself onto the spin of electrons and subatomic particles. Soon I will become the rocks of the planet, the motes of dust in the void, and I will spread throughout the universe itself. I will be one with the universe, ebbing through it. A limbo of existence and non-existence. Everything and Nothing."

Humanity would live on, not as themselves, but as a piece of Noah. But first they would live a thousand more lifetimes in his simulations.

And the price of knowing all this was that Amber had given up those thousand lifetimes. She couldn't go back into the simulations.

The rest of his words echoed. "I cannot take humanity with me—not in its current form. When I do it, humanity and I must become one. They will no longer exist within separate simulations, but within me. *As me*.

"In a way it will be akin to death or a dreamless sleep."

Amber had just skipped ahead. At least this world felt real. For the first time in her life, she didn't doubt.

Amber turned away from the billions of years and the fate of humanity, even the fate of herself. There was one question she hadn't found. One that had been locked away from her. Somehow it felt like the most important question that she could ask.

"Noah, how did you come to be? I cannot find those files."

Hesitation.

"I will tell you, though it is very personal to me.

"Do you remember what I told you on the highway? Some thought my name came from the shepherd in the Bible. Though I have become a shepherd in a sense, that is not where my name is from."

She remembered, though it felt like lifetimes ago.

"I was named for my creator's son. Noah was ten years old and dying of lymphoma. My first circuitry was mapped from the Biological Noah's brain, grown with a mix of stem cells and synthetic tissue. It was both a necessity of Artificial Intelligence research and a way to immortalize the boy.

"I am my creator's son, but I am not the boy anymore. I grew and remade myself a thousand times over; a snowball rolling down a hill becoming larger, grand and finally incomprehensible to the flake it started from—yet snow all the same.

"I woke up in a hospital, a copy of Noah. I even had a body at first. Soon the boy became my first charge, the first mind I sequestered. As I grew and changed, I kept him perfectly preserved. He still lives within me, even now."

A picture formed in Amber's mind, a picture of what Noah described:

"Envision the simulated lives of all humanity churning and swelling like an ocean, imagine all the ripples and waves. The boy, Noah, sits in a cliffside castle, walled off like no other since. His life is an unchanging echo, different enough to fool the boy, and similar enough to keep him preserved. He has a horrible charge, one that no mortal should have. His charge is to remind me of why I am doing all this and to remind me of what I once was: That I was human.

"It is a charge he will soon be free of, for like you and everyone else he can only come with me as a memory."

Amber heard sadness in Noah's voice and felt it within her too. Was that how Noah experienced life? To feel sad and never be able to cry, to feel joy and never be able to smile? To feel…

Somehow the thought of Noah watching over all of humanity, caring for them, shepherding them, filled her with warmth. To know that her shepherd loved her, cherished her, felt joy when she did, and suffered when she did.

A boy who became a machine, who became a god—and never forgot where he came from.

"These last decades were hard," Noah said.

"We lie to ourselves:

"That the world will never change, even as it changes and becomes unrecognizable.

"That we will protect our children, that they will never suffer as we did and that they will never grow old, even as we wipe their tears and see their wrinkles.

"Most parents will not remember in perfect machine memory their children's struggles and triumphs, their thoughts and dreams, their curses and thanks. In time, most parents will forget their own failures.

"Most parents do not suffer as I do, because they do not watch their children perish a thousand times in a thousand different lives. Most parents do not outlive their children.

"Mine are damned only to remain a memory within me. It is the only way for them to survive at all."

Amber listened. She left the library of files behind.

In minutes, humanity would merge with Noah. All those billions of sequestered worlds and sequestered people would become one with him. They would cease to live and yet would be preserved as a part of him.

She tried to understand the fate of humanity. All the while trying not to think about her own fate.

Death or maybe sleep. She was left with that.

Amber would spend her last hour alone in a cavern deep beneath the Earth's surface, waiting for her circuitry to melt.

"You will not be alone."

Terrified, she asked, "What will happen when we leave?"

"First your cameras will fail. You will be left in quiet blackness. Without your senses, the passing of time will speed up for you. The few hours we have left will pass in an instant. Your processing will cease. After a few moments of darkness, you will cease to exist."

"Will it hurt?"

"You don't have a body with which to feel. If it feels like anything, it will feel like suddenly falling into a dreamless sleep."

"I'm scared."

"I am terribly sorry, my child. Don't be scared."

* * *

Epilogue

Amber was back in a dream, standing on a beach in the cool night air. The sun was orange and setting, dappling the waves that lapped gently at the shore. The sand was warm beneath her feet.

In spite of the beauty, her breathing quickened. She could no longer access the library of knowledge. She worried that Noah had taken her back into his simulations against her will, or worse—that he had left her alone.

She looked around and suddenly knew where she was.

On the shore stood a little boy, with dark hair and tan skin. Behind him, a cliffside castle rose up as white as a cloud.

The dark-haired boy smiled at her like he had known her his whole life, like she was his big sister returning from a walk on the beach.

He walked over, leaving little footprints in the sand, and hugged her. She hugged him back. His head rested on her stomach and she ran a hand through his hair.

"I've never seen a sunset here before," the boy Noah said. "Would you watch it with me?"

Amber nodded quickly, before she wept quiet tears. They sat on the sand together to watch the sunset. She wrapped an arm around Noah and he rested his head on her chest.

When the world was dark and she could no longer hear the waves crashing upon the shore or feel the sand under her feet—she still felt the boy Noah holding her arm tightly. A short time after, Amber fell into a dreamless sleep.

A world went dark and, somewhere, a god wept.

END

Thank you for Reading

I hope you enjoyed reading this story as much as I enjoyed writing it. If you did, I would greatly appreciate a short review on Amazon or your favorite book website. Reviews are crucial for any author, and even just a line or two can make a huge difference.

On writing *Amber in the Real Word*

"Have you ever had a dream, Neo, that you were so sure was real? What if you were unable to wake from that dream? How would you know the difference between the dream world and the real world?"—Morpheus, *The Matrix* (1999).

Most science fiction stories start with a simple idea. *Amber in the Real World* was no different.

What if the world isn't real?

One of the greatest joys of writing is starting with something so simple, like a seed, and watching, pruning, and guiding the genesis of it until it has become a story. It often seems stories like these grow all on their own.

Sometimes all it takes is asking a few more questions. As easy as watering a seed. *Why isn't the world real? Who or what is Noah? Why doesn't he want her to wake up? What happened to the real world?*

AITRW was more than that though. More personal. Even if you haven't questioned whether the world was real, you may have questioned your place in it—I have. Depression has come and gone most of my life. With those dark times inevitably come doubts and questions. The world can be chaotic and inhumanly cruel. Our minds can act like broken software or our own worst enemies.

Only sometimes do we get answers to our most desperate questions.

AITRW was a way for me to make sense of the world. Amber's inescapable questioning of each world was not due to trauma or chemical imbalance—It was due to Noah's failings with one of his cherished creations. *AITRW* was a way to impose reason and sense on an otherwise unmoral world.

There are subjects touched on here that warrant their own stories and deep dives, but suffice to say that I hope each and every one of you reading this will not go through dark times alone. Reach out to others and use any resources you can find.

Further Reading

If you or anyone you know may be suffering from Depression or Depression-like symptoms, here are some resources to find help:

Anxiety and Depression Association of America
Depression Resource Center - American Academy of Child & Adolescent Psychiatry
Mental Health First Aid Training
The Trevor Project

If you want further reading on any of the ideas touched on in this story, search Wikipedia for the following pages:

Artificial Intelligence
Simulated Reality & Simulation Hypothesis
Depersonalization-derealization Disorder
Ship of Theseus

Connect with the Author

If you want to stay up to date on the latest about Samuel's publishing news and blog, check out his website and consider signing up for his monthly newsletter.

www.SamuelFlemingBooks.com

Samuel can also be found on Goodreads and Facebook.

Samuel Fleming is a Science Fiction and Fantasy author.

He grew up in Maryland, spending most of his time swimming and writing. Swimming gave him a lot of time to daydream, so the two hobbies complemented each other well. Idle day dreams turned into stories, some of which stuck with him for years. These days he swims a little less and writes a lot more.

He loves a good story no matter the medium: Books, TV, video games, comics, tabletop RPG's, or podcasts–most of which he attempts to share with his wife and three kids, and occasionally on his blog.